# Firestarter

## Contents

# OXFORD
## UNIVERSITY PRESS

Great Clarendon Street, Oxford OX2 6DP

Oxford University Press is a department of the University of Oxford. It furthers the University's objective of excellence in research, scholarship, and education by publishing worldwide in

Oxford  New York

Auckland  Cape Town  Dar es Salaam  Hong Kong  Karachi
Kuala Lumpur  Madrid  Melbourne  Mexico City  Nairobi
New Delhi  Shanghai  Taipei  Toronto

With offices in

Argentina  Austria  Brazil  Chile  Czech Republic  France  Greece
Gautamala  Hungary  Italy  Japan  South Korea  Poland  Portugal
Singapore  Switzerland  Thailand  Turkey  Ukraine  Vietnam

Oxford is a registered trade mark of Oxford University Press
in the UK and in certain other countries

Text © Judith Kneen 2008

The moral rights of the author have been asserted

Database right Oxford University Press (maker)

First published 2008

British Library Cataloguing in Publication Data

Data available

ISBN 978 019 832854 4

10 9 8 7 6 5 4 3 2 1

Printed in China by Printplus

## Acknowledgements

The Publisher would like to thank the following for permission to reproduce photographs:

P1t: Dale O'Dell/Alamy; P1tl: Oxford University Press; p1b: Phil Rees/Alamy; p3: Catherine Forde; p5tr: Oxford University Press; p5tl: iStock/Oxford University Press; p5b: Rex Argent/Alamy; p6: Oxford University Press; p7: Oxford University Press; p10l: Dale O'Dell/Alamy; p10r: Trevor Payne/Alamy; p11: Phil Rees/Alamy; p15b: Oliver Burston/Egmont UK Ltd;

Illustrations are by Steve Evans.
Cover artwork on p4 is by Cliff Nielsen.

Cover illustration by Oliver Burston

We are grateful for permission to reprint the following copyright material in this guide:

Paul Cruickshank: book review of *Firestarter*, used by permission of the author.

Catherine Forde: extracts from *Firestarter* (Egmont, 2006) and letters to Editor, reprinted by permission of Egmont UK Ltd; letter and notes, reprinted by permission of the author.

Mal Peet & Elspeth Graham: book review of *Firestarter*, used by permission of the authors

HowStuffWorks.com: extract from 'How Fire Works' at www.science.howstuffworks.com/fire

David McCall: notes about arson, used by permission of the author.

John Mannion: book review of *Firestarter*, used by permission of the author.

We have tried to trace and contact all copyright holders before publication. If notified, the publishers will be pleased to rectify any errors or omissions at the earliest opportunity.

*Firestarter*

# A Letter from Catherine Forde

Hello Reader,

In the two books I wrote before *Firestarter* (*Fat Boy Swim* and *SKARRS*) the central male teenage characters have massive problems to deal with. As the mother of teenage boys myself I know that many – maybe even most teenage boys – don't have such huge problems. So I decided make the central character in my next book more normal and well adjusted, with a stable, happy family background. However, when you make a straightforward teenager like Keith your central character in a novel that brings about another problem: he's a decent guy but his hassle-free life is pretty boring to write and read about. That's why, very early into *Firestarter* I had to inject some drama, excitement, danger. A problem…

It's all there in the character of Reece. There's absolutely nothing straightforward or normal about him. His arrival shakes Keith's world to its foundations. Reece literally walks into Keith's life and turns it upside down in the space of a week.

Where did Reece come from? Well, I wanted to create someone who couldn't always tell right from wrong. Everything about Reece had to be out of the ordinary, from his anti-social behaviour to his distinctive appearance. His look was inspired by the incredible video for The Prodigy's 'Firestarter'. Like the very best music videos this one is a phenomenal work of art: a perfect marriage of image and music. The sight of painted, studded Keith Flint snarling lyrics straight to camera creates something sinister and full of menace, yet it's also mesmerizing and unforgettable. I decided to make my problem character a Firestarter. I sent him up Keith's garden path, lit the touch paper, stood back and watched it catch fire.

I'd love to know what you feel about Reece when you meet him in *Firestarter*. By the end of the story will you agree with Keith's mum who says 'sometimes people are plain bad'. Or, like Annie and – to a lesser extent – like Keith, will you warm to Reece? (Pardon the pun.) Whatever your opinion, I hope you enjoy the story.

Cathy Forde

# Fire: Images and Words

## Images of fire

The image of fire can be used as a metaphor or simile. It can help to describe an idea or feeling, e.g. 'Her heart was ablaze', 'The rumour spread like wildfire'.

◎ Look at the ideas and feelings in the fire below.
◎ Create a simile or metaphor linked to fire for each one.
◎ With a partner, share your ideas. Discuss how well each one works and choose your favourite.

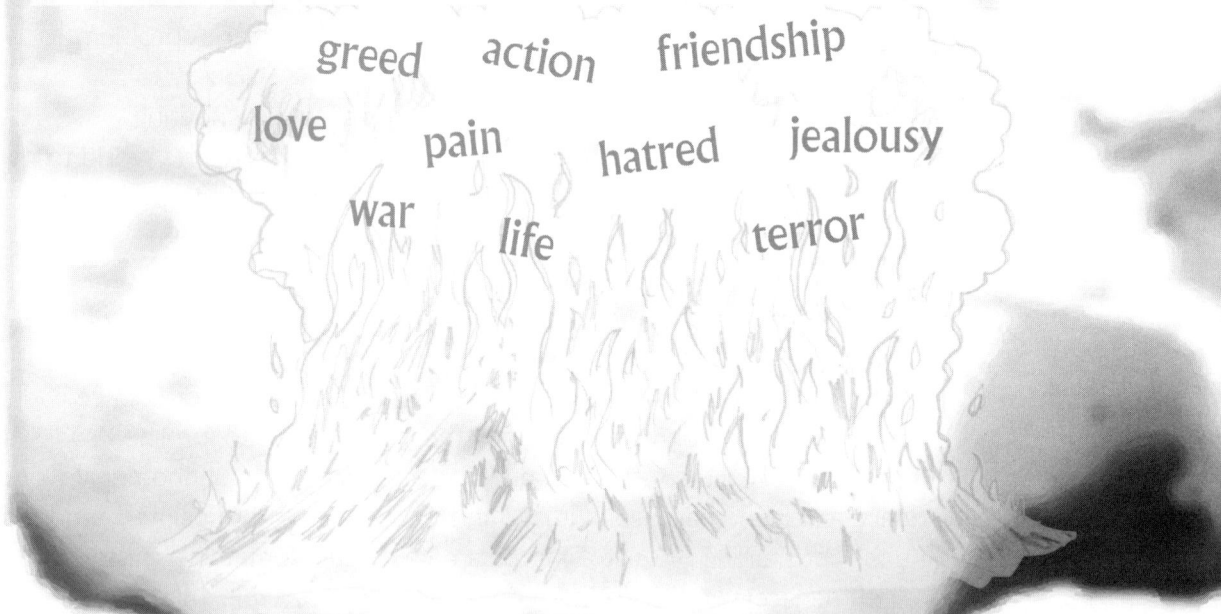

greed    action    friendship
love    pain    hatred    jealousy
war    life    terror

## Songs of fire

Fire is found in proverbs (well-known sayings that state a truth), e.g. 'There's no smoke without fire'. It is also often featured in song titles and lyrics.

◎ Do an Internet search for songs using the word fire, e.g. www.poemhunter.com/songs/fire/
◎ Analyse some of the songs to see how and why fire is used as a metaphor.

Read the words in the word bank below. Use them to create your own poems or song lyrics featuring fire as an image or theme.

## Judging a book by its cover

Look at the title and the front cover of *Firestarter*. What do you think it will be about? What ideas and feelings might be raised in this story?

ashes beating burning cool danger
desire destroy die dust eyes falling
fear fire flame heat hot light love
pain red starter sun tempting
trouble truth twisted warm wild

# Who Are You?

## Youth culture

Youth culture first emerged in the 1950s and 60s with mods, rockers and hippies. Today, there are a whole host of ways in which young people categorize themselves and each other, for example emo, hip-hop, goth, and chav.

Appearance and music are the two big indicators of youth image, but other things can be important too, such as books, films, art and language.

◎ Discuss why groupings can be important to young people.
◎ Match each label to the right description, below.

| Labels | Descriptions |
| --- | --- |
| goth | The roots of this group are in urban African American youth. Key elements include rapping, DJ-ing and graffiti. |
| hip-hopper | Dyed black hair, black clothes, heavy makeup and silver jewellery are typical elements of this group's appearance. |
| punk | This group likes rock and roll music, wearing leather jackets and riding classic motorbikes. |
| rocker | This group started in the late 1970s. They enjoy loud, raucous music and shocking fashions, including the Mohican haircut. |

## First impressions

These words describe a character in the novel, called Reece:

'matted blue hair, all spiked up and red at the tips'     'a studded leather collar'

'a face painted half black, half white'     'shredded black clothes'

'steel-tipped Docs...'     'draped in chains'

◎ Draw a rough sketch of Reece, using the descriptions.
◎ What do the descriptions reveal about Reece and the type of person he might be?

*Firestarter*

# Character Profiles

## MyPlace *on the Net*

### Keith's place - welcome!

### Fact file

**Name:** Keith
**Nickname:** Teef
**Age:** 16
**Looks:** people say I'm short but I reckon I'm perfect
**Like:** my little sister – she's a real cute sprog
**Hate:** dogs – well ones like the mad one that nearly ate me recently
**Favourite food:** pizza with my mates
**Favourite place:** Scotland

<u>More about me</u>

### About me

Okay – so I guess I'm Mr Sensible, but somebody's got to be. I get on with my parents, I think my little sister, Annie, is adorable and I like my Gran (although her dog is a bit of a stinker). I don't have any big hang-ups about growing up and don't get into trouble. But it's not a crime you know – being perfect! It's just who I am. Bit of a soft touch I suppose….

<u>Click here to read more</u>

### My blog

The holidays start tomorrow. And I've got the perfect job – lounging around at home and getting paid for it. I've just got to look after a three-year-old sprog – can't be that hard can it?

<u>Click here to read more</u>

### My mates

**Stewball** – 6 foot giant with karate black belt – no messing with him then! Gone to Florida – lucky so-and-so.
**Stevie** – Another big lump of a bloke – but all dotey about Annie!

<u>Click here for messages from my mates</u>

<u>My music</u>          <u>My pics</u>          <u>My videos</u>

This is Keith's page on a social networking site.
◎ What does it reveal about his character?
◎ The underlined text shows links to other web pages. Write some of the other pages on Keith, revealing more about him from what you've read in the story and from what you can imagine.

*Firestarter*

# MyPlace *on the Net*

## FIRESTARTER!

### Fact file

**Name:** Reece
**Nickname:** Firestarter
**Age:** 15
**Looks:** some people say 'striking'
– just like a match! I say
– once seen, never forgotten!
**Like:** shopping without money
**Hate:** interfering old relatives
**Favourite food:** anything hot
**Favourite place:** sitting by a fire,
gazing at the
flames

<u>More about me</u>

### About me

I'm the firestarter. A survivor. Travelling from place to place, in and out of trouble, but I'm too smart for them. They'll never pin things on me – I'm too quick, too fit, too sharp.

You have to look out for yourself when you have no mother. It makes you hard and tough. I'm a softy when it comes to animals though – some people just don't know how to treat their pets.

<u>Click here to read more</u>

### My blog

Keith is my new mate. Lives next door behind a huge fence. He doesn't really know me well yet. He's a bit wary because I look different or maybe my duff old aunt has said something to him but he'll warm to me. His sister's a real sweetie. Finally, I've found some friends and I think we're going to get on like a house on fire…

<u>Click here to read more</u>

<u>My music</u>            <u>My pics</u>            <u>My videos</u>

Reece also has pages on MyPlace. His home page is above.

◎ What do we learn about Reece?

◎ What do we learn about the differences between Reece and Keith?

◎ Write some of the other pages on Reece, revealing more about him from what you've read in the story and from your imagination.

# People and Places

## No place called home

This story is set in Glasgow. It is Keith's permanent home and Reece's current home.

◎ On the map are some places mentioned in the novel. In which of them has Reece lived? (See pages 59 and 69.)

◎ What effect might living in so many places have on Reece?

◎ Improvise the arrival of Reece in one of the different places, perhaps his first day with foster parents or his first day at a new school. Think carefully about how he might feel, what sort of image he might try to convey and how other people might respond to him.

## Local lingo

Keith is Scottish and, as the writer tells the story through Keith, he uses Scottish dialect words.

Look at the words below and where they come from in the story. Then match them up to the correct meaning on the right.

| Scottish dialect | Page |
|---|---|
| aye | 4 |
| gives it laldy | 8 |
| scoosh-case | 21 |
| foosty | 26 |
| shoogling | 33 |
| footering | 35 |
| bampot | 40 |

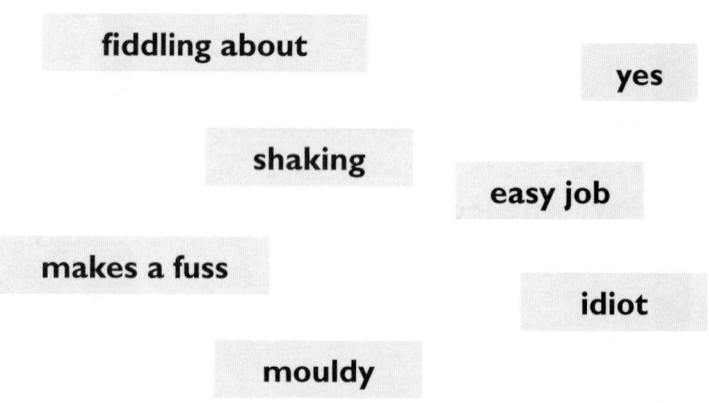

fiddling about

yes

shaking

easy job

makes a fuss

idiot

mouldy

## Keith's voice

As well as dialect, the writer uses other ways to establish Keith's voice and viewpoint:

◎ slang words (e.g. 'chuffed', page 3)

◎ talking directly to the reader ('So now you know why Annie's precious', page 5)

◎ humour ('I'd need to be Annie's flipping superhero, zooming from the clouds in spangly lycra and a magic cape…', page 4)

◎ short sentences ('I'm on duty now. Clocked on', page 1).

Find more examples of each in the story. Discuss their effect and how they make us feel about Keith.

*Firestarter*

# Piecing Together the Story

The events of the story take place over the course of a week. Each chapter deals with one day. This gives the novel a clear, simple structure. It also helps to build tension for the reader, as it acts like a 'countdown' to the end of the week.

The documents below relate to some of the events that help to build up tension and suspense in the novel.

◎ Work out which chapters they all come from. (There is one for each day of the week.)

◎ Discuss how they add to the build up of tension and suspense.

**LADY**
If found,
return to address
on reverse

Dear Jean,
Reece has arrived but is proving a handful. I think I'm too old for looking after kids with problems. When the neighbour's boy called round this morning, I automatically thought that Reece was up to no good again, but this time at least I was wrong...

## Mario's — Perfect Pizza

| Pizza | 9" | 14" |
|---|---|---|
| Pepperoni | £4.99 | £6.99 |
| Margarita | £4.50 | £6.50 |
| Meat feast | £5.99 | £7.99 |
| Hawaiian | £5.99 | £7.99 |

Still at airport.
Flight delayed.
Stay away
from you know
who.
c u l8r. Dad

| D | M | 20__ | | Fire investigation report |

On arrival at the scene, the fire was well advanced. Extensive damage to the house had occurred. Our first priority was to rescue any occupants.

**Patient notes**

Smoke inhalation has led to considerable lung damage, but is now stable. Patient is still under sedation...

2007

Dear diary,
I feel so guilty – leaving them all for the week, but Keith's a good kid. He's responsible and I'd rather leave Annie with my son than anyone else...

# Facts about Fire

Here is some information about fire. Read it carefully.

## What is Fire?

The ancient Greeks considered fire one of the major elements in the universe, alongside water, earth and air. This grouping makes intuitive sense: You can feel fire, just like you can feel earth, water and air. You can also see it and smell it, and you can move it from place to place.

But fire is really something completely different. Earth, water and air are all forms of matter – they are made up of millions and millions of <u>atoms</u> collected together. Fire isn't matter at all. It's a visible, tangible side effect of matter **changing form** – it's one part of a **chemical reaction**.

Typically, fire comes from a chemical reaction between **oxygen** in the atmosphere and some sort of **fuel** (wood or <u>gasoline</u>, for example). Of course, wood and gasoline don't spontaneously catch on fire just because they're surrounded by oxygen. For the combustion reaction to happen, you have to heat the fuel to its **ignition temperature**.

The dangerous thing about the chemical reactions in fire is the fact that they are self-perpetuating. The heat of the flame itself keeps the fuel at the ignition temperature, so it continues to burn as long as there is fuel and oxygen around it. The flame heats any surrounding fuel so it releases gases as well. When the flame ignites the gases, the fire spreads.

From How Stuff Works – www.science.howstuffworks.com/fire

Fire is started naturally by volcanoes and lightning.

Some plant seeds will only germinate after fire, once the area has been cleared of competing plants.

## Find out...

Do some more research about fire. Choose two of the following topics to explore.

◎    How fire was traditionally started
◎    The story of Prometheus
◎    The invention of modern 'striking' matches.
◎    How to make different colour flames.

Think up two questions about fire for a partner to find answers to.
(Make sure you know the answers from your own research!)

*Firestarter*

# Fire Crime

## Fire Crime

All these names describe people who deliberately start fires: **fire bug, fire setter, arsonist, firestarter**.

Starting fires deliberately as a crime is called 'arson' in England and Wales, although not in Scotland. Catherine Forde (the author) wanted to ensure her story was accurate and plausible, so she researched the crime in Scottish law. Here is some information she was given by a police officer.

**New Message**

Send | Chat | Attach | Address | Fonts | Colors | Save As Draft

1. The crime of arson only applies in England and Wales. In Scotland the situation is a little trickier. If someone sets fire to a house or business premises for instance, the crime is the common law crime of wilful fireraising. This can be a very serious crime and tried in solomn procedure depending on the seriousness of the fire. For instance, was anyone killed or injured? How much damage was caused, etc.

2. Secondly, if someone sets fire to property such as a house or business but does so unintentionally and through otherwise criminal conduct (e.g. someone who makes a fire-bomb and throws it in the street but the net result is that the fire takes hold of a nearby building) the crime is reckless fireraising.

3. Lastly, if someone deliberately sets fire to an item of 'moveable property', e.g. a car or haystack, etc. the crime is malicious fireraising.

◎  Catherine Forde annotated the email. What words has she annotated and why?
◎  When you have read the whole book, decide what crime you think Reece has committed.

## Obsession

Hot-seat Reece about his obsession with fire. A volunteer should take on the role of Reece and the rest of the group/class ask him questions.

## Dilemma

Discuss the following question:
*Is Reece just a criminal who needs locking up, or a damaged boy who needs help?*

Firestarter

# The Birth of a Story

When she plans a book, Catherine Forde says 'I get a couple of sheets of paper and fill them up with ideas over a few weeks before I start writing'. Below, you can see some of her planning notes for *Firestarter*.

◎   Discuss what these notes tell us about how she plans. You may want to consider: length, how and why she emphasizes points, the dialogue she has with herself.

◎   Such brief notes can emphasize the main intentions and messages of a writer.  What do you think are her messages about Reece?

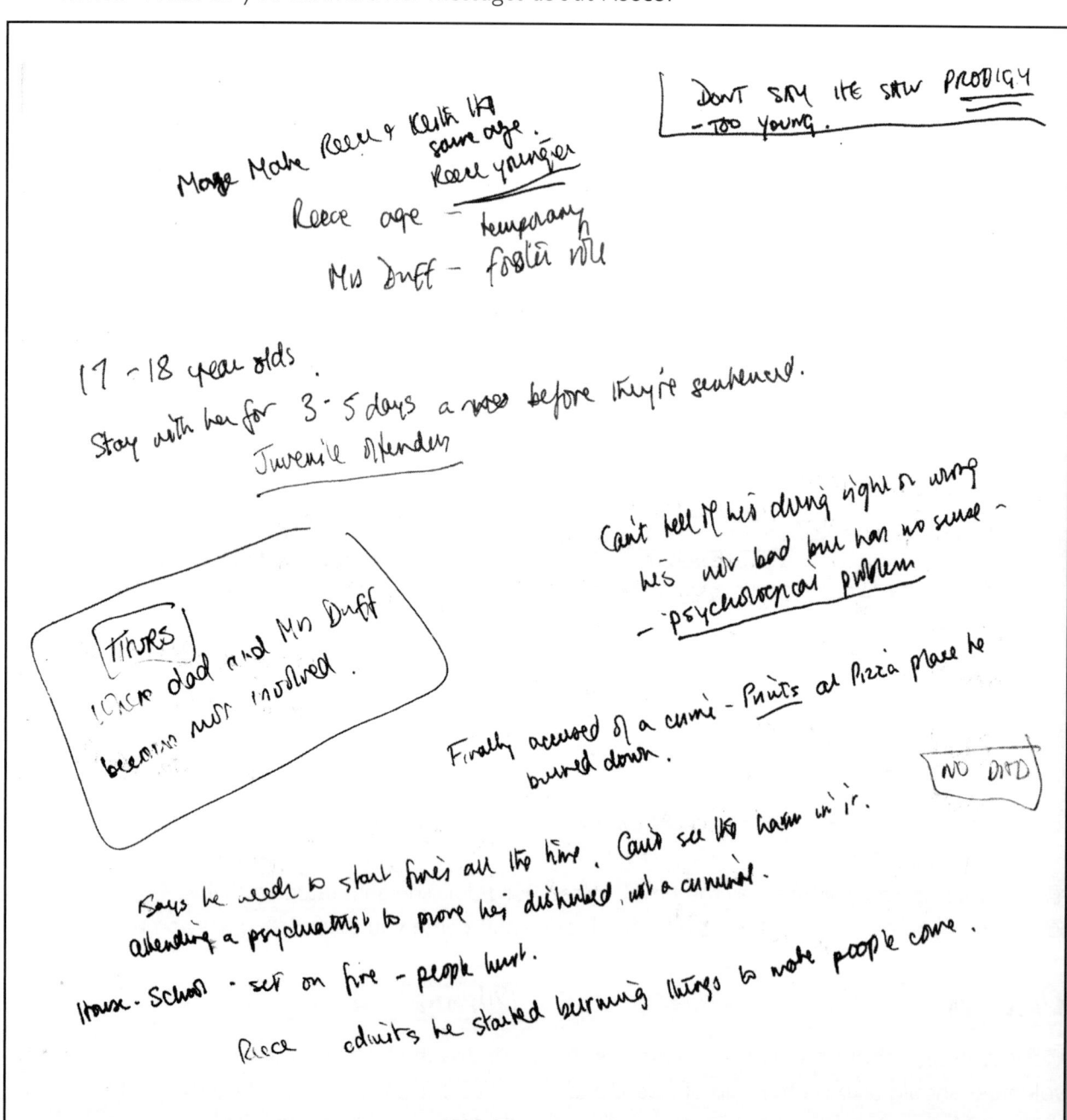

# the Editor's Job

A writer works with an editor who helps to prepare the story for publication. Here are some comments from Catherine Forde's editor about an early draft of the story.

**A**

... I think what's most exciting about *Firestarter* is that whilst it has all the emotional depth and powerful characterisation of *Fat Boy Swim* and *Skarrs* it is very different in tone and pace. Taut, claustrophobic, chilling, *Firestarter* is a griping psychological thriller. Like the most effective horror stories, what makes it so powerful is the ordinary domestic setting turned upside down by the nightmare neighbour. It's a situation any reader could imagine. However, because you are such an intelligent writer, *Firestarter* is so much more than a thriller; it is an exploration of our perception of evil, and it challenges the attitudes of those who claim to worry about the plight of alienated teenagers – as long as they don't live on their back door.

**B**

Your characters hold us spellbound but what first grabs the attention is what you do with the tone and atmosphere of the book. At the beginning you give readers the impression they are about to enjoy a comedy about a teenage boy looking after a baby. Then the tone starts to change on page 9, becoming sinister and claustrophobic and distinctly uncomfortable. At times, very cleverly, you manage to walk the fine line between horror and comedy, for example, Keith and Reece bickering over the repair job Keith has done on Raggy (page 50).
Your writing is as sensuous and atmospheric as ever. So many images and sounds stay with me, for example: the humour of Stevie half in Annie's Wendy house on page 6; the pathetic description of Mrs Duff on page 27; the chilling sound of Reece bashing his head against the wall on page 45; the fear in Annie on page 84. And then there is the assault on our olfactory senses with Gran and her farting dog, Reece and his stench of petrol and sulphur, and Mrs Duff and her cabbagey aroma.

**C**

A pedantic thought: if Dad is not much of a cook, wouldn't Mum leave pre-cooked meals?

**D**

Pedantry again: how could teenage Keith fit into three-year-old Annie's nurse outfit? Also, do teenage boys watch ER? Of course, you're far more likely to know that than I am!

◎ What is the purpose of an editor? What jobs does he or she do?
◎ What does Extract A tell us about the relationship between this editor and author?
◎ The page numbers refer to a draft and not the published novel. How many of the references mentioned in Extract B can you find in the novel?
◎ In Extracts C and D, the editor gives very specific advice. Can you find evidence in the story as to how Catherine Forde responded to it?

*Firestarter*

# Reviews

Here are some extracts from reviews of Firestarter.

Keith is that rare thing in teen fiction: a good sensible kid with no chip on his shoulder and no dreadful problems – until Reece shows up. The central conflict seems, at first, to be between Keith's 'goodness' and Reece's 'badness'; Forde gradually undermines this simplistic perception in an unpreachy and unlaboured way.

*(From a review by Mal Peet and Elspeth Graham)*

Another well-handled aspect of the novel is the process in which Keith is drawn into Reece's world by a combination of embarrassment, sympathy and lack of assertiveness. Keith is by no means a hero but by the same token Reece is not simply presented as a villain.

*(From a review by John Mannion)*

The splitting of the story into the seven days of the week drives it on quite forcefully. There's a sense of terrible inevitability surrounding the behaviour of the arsonist Reece: the reader knows disaster is ahead but it's our predictions as to what awful event is destined that gives the story pace and excitement.

*(From a review by Paul Cruickshank)*

*Firestarter makes for a compulsive, chilling read. The spare, simple style you have chosen is highly successful: a taut, suspenseful plot develops at a fire-licking pace, and the focus on the relationship between Keith and Reece is mesmerizing. It is claustrophobic and tense, almost unbearably tense.*

*(From a letter by Catherine Forde's editor)*

◎ Which review(s) focus on:
  - character
  - style
  - structure
  - a central idea or theme?
◎ Discuss whether or not you agree with these reviewers.
◎ Write your own review of *Firestarter*. Apart from the areas above, you might include comments on:
  - the opening
  - the language
  - the setting
  - the most effective/least effect parts.

*Firestarter*

# Promotion

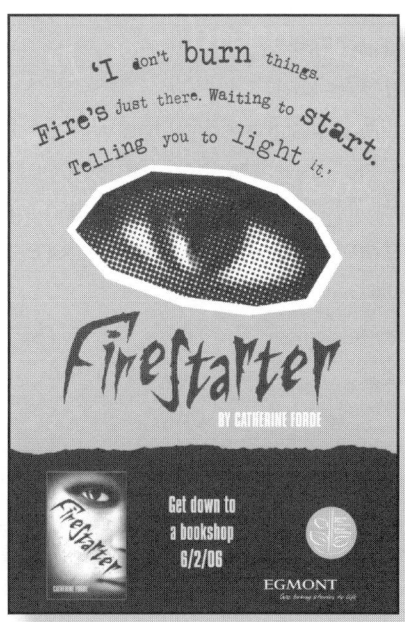

Posters promoting Firestarter were put up at skate parks.

The cover of the first edition of Firestarter.

◎ Discuss how the novel has been promoted, for example:
 - how the images attract the reader
 - what the images reveal about the content
 - what makes the cover distinctive
 - the style of font used
 - what kind(s) of reader the book aimed at.

◎ The book was promoted at skate parks. Why do you think this type of venue was chosen?

◎ Imagine you are responsible for marketing the novel. You have been asked to consider fresh ways of promoting it. Prepare a presentation, including your plans and designs.

Possible ideas to consider:
 - new venues
 - competitions
 - type of media (e.g. TV, radio, websites)
 - special events.

A poster promoting Firestarter.

# Pathways... to Another Good Read

## Works by the same author

*Fat Boy Swim*
ISBN 9-781405-202398
Because he is overweight, Jimmy hides his culinary talents. After all it will just make kids tease him more. But Jimmy is about to prove a lot more to himself that he didn't expect.

*The Drowning Pond*
ISBN 1-40522-176-3
Some girls will stop at nothing to be popular. This novel explores just how badly wrong things can go.

*Skarrs*
ISBN 9-781405-209472
Danny is a mixed-up teenager. He is linked up with the dangerous and racist Jakey, and likes listening to the violent lyrics of his favourite band, the Skarrs. Then he learns something startling about his dead 'Grampa' which makes him think again.

## Thematically-linked texts

*The Tulip Touch*
by Anne Fine
ISBN 978-014132047-2
Natalie is fascinated by the wild and dangerous Tulip, but then she finds herself out of her depth. This book looks at what happens when a disadvantaged girl goes bad. There are significant parallels with *Firestarter*.

*Kit's Wilderness*
by David Almond
ISBN 978-044041605-0
A powerful story, told with Almond's trademark simplicity. It is a tale of the unlikely friendship of two boys: sensitive Kit and the more dominant Askew. Kit is the narrator.

*The Other Side of Truth*
by Beverley Naidoo
ISBN 978-043512530-1
Losing your mother is traumatic and means the world can become a hostile place. This book tells the story of how two children survive after the murder of their mother.

*The Same Stuff as Stars*
by Katherine Paterson
ISBN 978-019832632-8
Taking responsibility for a younger sibling brings a world of responsibility, as Angel discovers when her mother dumps her with her great-grandma.

*Beast*
by Ally Kennan
ISBN 0-439-95104-6
Stephen, a teenage boy in foster care, has a terrifying secret – a secret that is growing more dangerous by the day. Can he rid himself of this extraordinary beast which threatens his whole world?

*Daydreamer*
by Ian McEwan
ISBN 0-099-47071-3
This book provides an extraordinary glimpse into the creative mind of a ten-year-old boy, which includes a horror scene involving dolls.

*Firestarter*